BEASTQUEST

→ BOOK EIGHT ←

CLAW
THE GIANT APE

ADAM BLADE

ILLUSTRATED BY EZRA TUCKER

SCHOLASTIC INC.

New York Toronto London Auckland Sydney
Mexico City New Delhi Hong Kong Buenos Aires

With special thanks to Lucy Courtenay
For my very own Beasts, Alfie and George

ISBN-13: 978-0-545-06864-2
ISBN-10: 0-545-06864-9

Beast Quest series created by Working Partners Ltd., London.
BEAST QUEST is a trademark of Working Partners Ltd.

12 11 10 9 8 7 6 5 4 3   9 10 11 12 13/0

Designed by Tim Hall
Printed in the U.S.A.
First printing, September 2008

Did you think it was over?

Did you think I would accept defeat and disappear?

No! That can never be. I am Malvel, the Dark Wizard who strikes fear into the hearts of the people of Avantia. I still have much more to show this wretched kingdom, and one boy in particular — Tom.

The young hero liberated the six Beasts of Avantia from my curse. But his fight is far from over. Let us see how he fares with a new Quest, one that will surely crush him and his companion, Elenna.

Avantia's Beasts had good hearts that I corrupted for my own wicked purpose. Now, thanks to Tom, they are free to protect the kingdom once more. But I have created new supreme Beasts whose hearts are evil and so cannot be set free. Each one guards a piece of the most precious relic of Avantia, a relic I have stolen: the suit of golden armor that gives magical strength to its rightful owner. I will stop at nothing to prevent Tom from collecting the complete suit and defeating me again. This time he will not win!

Malvel

THE AIR WAS HOT AND HUMID. THE MARKET trader mopped his brow and stared into the thick mass of jungle trees before him. They reminded him of rotten black teeth. Heavy vines hung down like snakes.

"Do we have to go in there?" asked the boy at the trader's side. "Is there no other way?"

"We've traveled hundreds of miles for the Ruby Guya fruit," the trader reminded his assistant. "It grows nowhere else in Avantia. Only here in the Dark Jungle."

"But aren't there monsters who live in there? That's what people say," the boy whispered.

"Rumors to frighten honest men," said the trader with a wave of his hand.

"Is it true the Ruby Guya possesses miraculous powers?" the boy asked.

The trader nodded. "One bite of its sweet red flesh brings courage to the fainthearted and strength to the weak," he said. "It is only ever seen at the king's table, and fetches a price greater than rubies." He glanced at his young assistant. "But we must keep our heads if we are to harvest it. Do you understand?"

The boy swallowed his fear and nodded.

They entered the jungle side by side. At once the light grew dim. Birds screamed and wheeled overhead. Great tree ferns arched above them, their leaves a bright and poisonous green.

The trader gazed at the fleshy jungle flowers that hung in ropes from the trees. They smelled over-ripe and dangerous. He forced all thoughts of deadly creatures and scents from his mind. But he couldn't shake the feeling that something was watching them.

A branch crashed to the ground. The trader whirled, pulling his knife from its sheath in one swift movement. But all he saw were the trembling shadows of leaves.

They walked on. Soon they found themselves wading through a foul-smelling swamp. The thick, pungent water lapped at their knees. The trader clenched his teeth to stop them from trembling. Who knew what vile creatures lurked at his feet?

He wanted to weep with relief when they touched solid ground again.

"We must press on," he said.

The boy crawled out of the swamp. "Leeches," he sobbed. "They are all over me!"

The trader pried the leeches from the boy's bare ankles with the blade of his knife. Shuddering, he did the same to the bloodsuckers on his own limbs. The Dark Jungle was a terrible, stinking place. He would be glad to leave — once he found what he sought.

They moved on. Splashes of sunlight dripped to the ground like venom. Monkeys chattered in the highest treetops above them. It sounded as if they were laughing.

At last, through the ferns, the trader glimpsed a cluster of trees with green, waxy leaves and plump red fruits. His heart leaped.

The Ruby Guya!

The trader hauled himself to the nearest tree, laughing with delight.

"Come on, boy!" he called behind him. "This fruit is ripe for the picking. Where are you?"

He looked back over his shoulder. The boy had disappeared. Uneasy now, the trader glanced around the clearing. Something wasn't right.

There was a scuffling sound in the under-growth — and then a scream. The trader froze.

Suddenly, a gnarled claw shot out of the foliage and grabbed the fruit from the trader's hand. The man screamed as a hairy face with bloodshot eyes emerged from behind the green leaves. Huge lips curled back to reveal pointed, yellow teeth.

"Boy!" the trader croaked. "Run!"

Slowly, the trader looked back at the Beast. It was too late for escape. He howled as a long, thick tail with a deadly claw on its tip flicked out and wrapped itself around his waist.

The trader's screams echoed around the jungle clearing. Then he was gone.

CHAPTER ONE

CROSSING THE WINDING RIVER

Tom guided his black stallion, Storm, inland, away from Avantia's western shore. Elenna sat behind him, her arms around his waist. Silver, Elenna's pet wolf, padded quietly alongside. Struggling with Zepha the Monster Squid had been their toughest challenge yet. If it hadn't been for Sepron, the protector of Avantia's waters, they might never have defeated the evil Beast.

In one of Storm's saddlebags lay a magnificent golden helmet, shaped like the head of an eagle. It was the first piece he had recovered from the great suit of golden armor, which gave magical powers to its rightful owner. The armor had belonged to the Master of the Beasts and had been destined to pass to Tom as a reward for completing his first Quest. Now it was Tom's fate to recover the six pieces which had been stolen by the Dark Wizard Malvel and scattered across Avantia. But Malvel had created new evil Beasts to protect each piece. Zepha had been the first, with the helmet as his prize. There were still more Beasts to overcome before the remaining pieces of armor could be retrieved.

But that was not all. For Malvel had taken more than the armor. He had kidnapped Aduro, King Hugo's wizard and Tom and Elenna's friend and protector.

"I'm worried about Aduro," Elenna said.

"That's why we have to find and defeat this next Beast, Claw. Whatever he is," said Tom. "We will soon find all the pieces of the armor and, when our

Quest is complete, we will rescue Aduro. As he told us himself, there's no other way!"

Silver yapped in excitement, and Storm tossed his fine head.

"Malvel may have Aduro," said Tom, "but we still have Aduro's enchanted map. Let's see if it shows us the way to Claw."

They dismounted and Tom drew the parchment scroll from one of the saddlebags. As he unrolled it, the map sprang to life. The mountains of Avantia rose as high as his thumb and tiny waves crashed on the map's shores. Tom and Elenna shared a smile. No matter how many times they used the magical map, it never failed to amaze them.

Slowly the image on the map began to slide, revealing new terrain in the south. The landscape grew greener. A glowing red line appeared from Avantia's western shore and snaked down, past the

Winding River, into a small patch of deep green in the southeast.

"I have an idea where we might be headed," said Elenna, frowning. "There's a place called the Dark Jungle. . . ."

"I've heard the stories," Tom said. "Hot and dangerous, with dark shadows, poisonous plants, and spiders the size of your head. I've heard that if the heat and the insects don't kill you, the creatures will."

Elenna shuddered. "And that's *without* Malvel's Beast."

Tom studied the map more closely. Something was moving in the depths of the Dark Jungle. It glimmered, then disappeared again.

"Look," Tom said, showing Elenna the map. "Can you see? That tiny gold dot. Look closely."

"It's the chain mail!" Elenna said in excitement. "The next piece of the armor!"

Tom rolled up the map. "We're going to the Dark Jungle," he said. "There's no time to lose!"

Tom, Elenna, Storm, and Silver headed toward the Winding River. With the sun on their backs and wonderful views of Avantia all around them, it was easy to forget the danger of their Quest.

They followed the road down into a green valley. Tom studied their position on the map, tracing the red line toward the Dark Jungle.

When he had looked the first time, the tiny golden chain mail had been near the mouth of the jungle. Now it was deep among the trees.

Had Malvel moved it?

Tom's heart thumped.

Did he know they were coming?

They carried on. The road led deep into the valley. Soon Tom and Elenna could see the gleaming ribbon of water that was the Winding River. The riverbank twisted and turned like a writing snake, and the water glowed gold in the late-afternoon sun. The road stopped abruptly at the river's edge and there was no sign of a bridge. Up close, the water roared past them, wild and foaming. It looked dangerous.

Carefully, Tom took the golden eagle helmet from one of the saddlebags. It shone in the sunlight as if it were made of fire. His heart beating fast, Tom raised it above his head and slowly pulled it down over his face.

At once, his eyesight sharpened. He could see every blade of grass along the riverbank and, when he looked downstream, he saw the river stretching away for miles. Everything was crystal clear.

"Can you see anything?" Elenna asked.

"I can see *everything*," Tom said in wonder. "It's amazing! But I can't see a bridge."

"The river twists away behind those trees," said Elenna, pointing upstream. "Perhaps there is a bridge somewhere out of sight."

They followed the river upstream. Tom began to feel worried. The light was fading and they had to cross the water before nightfall.

They rounded another twist in the river. Silver barked.

"There!" Elenna shouted.

At last, a bridge.

But it looked old. The planks were warped, rickety, and broken in several places. Some were missing entirely, like teeth in an old witch's mouth. The water swirled below, white and furious.

"It won't take our weight if we cross together," said Tom, jumping from Storm. "But if we go one at a time, we might make it. Elenna, take Silver over first."

But Silver didn't need any help. In three bounds, the wolf was across. The bridge creaked and swayed, but stayed in one piece.

Tom gave Elenna an encouraging nod as she stepped on to the bridge. One of the planks cracked and fell into the water as she leaped for the shore. But she had made it.

"Come on, Storm," Tom coaxed, trying to sound confident. "You next."

But the stallion was spooked by the swirling water and refused to move.

Tom stepped onto the bridge, testing the plank with his weight. The twisted wood creaked under his feet, but didn't break.

"Come on, boy," Tom called softly, holding out his hand.

The stallion stepped forward. The wooden slats groaned in protest and the bridge swayed. Storm rolled his eyes in terror as Tom struggled to keep his calm and urge the horse forward.

A rotten plank snapped just as Storm's last back hoof lifted from it. Then the entire section of the bridge they had been standing on crumbled into the angry, churning water below.

"We need to lighten the load," Tom called over his shoulder to Elenna. Very slowly, he sank to his knees to spread his weight. Then he unfastened his helmet, shield, and sword.

"Catch!"

The bridge groaned again as Tom threw everything toward Elenna. Now he had no magic to protect him. Only his wits.

Tom edged forward, but the planks splintered. He could only watch in horror as the bridge began to fall away.

"Come on, Storm!" he shouted, scrambling toward the shore.

The stallion threw back his head and whinnied in terror as the bridge collapsed beneath him.

"No!" Elenna screamed from the bank.

But it was too late. Tom and Storm had fallen into the deadly water!

CHAPTER TWO

ORDEAL IN THE WATER

TOM FELT HIMSELF BEING DRAGGED UNDER THE surface. The water was cold and the current strong. Storm was panicking and thrashing his legs. With a lunge, Tom grabbed hold of the stallion's reins.

Half-blinded and choked by the water, he broke the surface of the river. "Throw me my sword!" he shouted to Elenna.

The heavy sword flew through the air and plunged into the water beside him. With a mighty effort, Tom reached out and grabbed hold of the hilt before the sword sank out of sight. His lungs were burning as he stabbed his sword into the riverbank with all his might and held on. The power of the current and Storm's weight almost dragged Tom away. But he kept his grip on the sword, and the blade held fast in the ground.

"Tom!" Elenna called, running to the edge of the river and holding out her hand.

He kicked hard, and felt solid ground just in front of him. His feet slithered through the mud, and the water sucked at his legs. Grunting with the effort, Tom grabbed Elenna's outstretched hand. Then he swung himself onto the bank and collapsed on the grass, sword in one hand and Storm's soaking leather reins in the other. But the horse was still struggling in the wild water, his hooves flailing.

"Pull with me, Elenna," Tom shouted.

Silver ran up and down the bank, barking and whining, as Elenna put her arms around Tom's waist and Tom leaned out to grab Storm's saddle.

Together they tried to drag Storm closer to the bank. But it was no good.

"Come on, Storm," Tom urged. His legs were trembling with exhaustion as he fell to his knees and gazed at his stallion.

Storm's eyes were wide and scared as the water rushed past him. He was beginning to lose the battle.

"Steady," Tom murmured, almost as if he were talking to himself. "Stay calm. Stay calm . . ."

He repeated the words over and over again, clicking his tongue, and gradually Storm's terrified eyes focused on him again.

Then, one step at a time, the stallion heaved himself through the water. At last, with a final, huge effort, he scrambled onto the riverbank.

Tom threw his arms around his horse. "Well done, Storm," he gasped, burying his face in the stallion's damp neck. He could feel himself grinning. "You did it, boy."

Elenna fell on Storm's neck and hugged the stallion fiercely. "Oh, Storm," she murmured. "I thought we'd lost you."

Snorting and blowing, Storm quieted. He nuzzled Tom gently as Elenna rushed to collect long grasses to dry the horse's flanks. They needed to get him dry — and warm — as quickly as possible.

As Tom unsaddled Storm and rubbed him with the grass, Elenna lit a campfire. Then Tom draped a blanket around the exhausted stallion. Storm swayed on his feet as if he were too tired to stand up for much longer. Then, gently, he sank to the ground beside the fire.

Quickly, Tom stripped off his wet clothes and wrapped himself in another blanket. His clothes would dry overnight beside the flames. Meanwhile, Silver brought Elenna a rabbit he had caught on the riverbank.

"Is the feast to your liking?" Tom joked, offering

Elenna a piece of bread and cheese as the rabbit roasted in the embers of the fire.

Elenna tore into the bread. "It'll do," she said between mouthfuls, and smiled.

Later Tom and Elenna ate the rabbit beside the crackling fire. The rushing sound of the water was comforting now. Tom lay back and stared at the night sky overhead. It was dotted with bright stars and the moon was almost full. His thoughts drifted to his father, Taladon, who had once undertaken a Beast Quest of his own. He wondered where he was now.

Then he realized that, at this moment, Elenna, Storm, and Silver were the closest thing to a family he had on this Quest. He never wanted to risk losing any of them again.

CHAPTER THREE

INTO THE DARK JUNGLE

THE NEXT MORNING DAWNED CLEAR AND STILL. To Tom's relief, Storm seemed rested and calm. Tom and Elenna breakfasted on fresh fish that Elenna caught in the waters of the Winding River. Silver bounded away as they ate, returning with another plump rabbit for himself, while Storm grazed on the short grasses nearby.

"Time to go," said Tom at last.

Elenna doused the fire and packed her belongings. Tom knew she was thinking about the Beast they were about to face. If he were honest, he was thinking about it as well. *What sort of a creature would Claw be?*

They soon found a road that led away from the Winding River. As they journeyed on, the valley walls grew steeper and the vegetation more lush. Silver ran ahead as clouds chased one another across the stripe of blue sky above.

After a while, the road dwindled to a stony track, potholed in places. It was clear that few people came this way. The thought made Tom feel uncomfortable. If the rumors about the Dark Jungle were true, what chance did they have of defeating Claw and finding the golden chain mail?

The stony track began to climb. Panting, Storm trudged up the steep incline, Silver padding quietly by his side. The sun beat down hard on Tom and Elenna's backs. The air felt close.

The track ended abruptly as they reached the top of a hill. Before them lay a sea of green trees. It stretched as far as the horizon.

"The Dark Jungle," Elenna said in awe. "It's bigger than I'd imagined."

The jungle was vast. Above the trees, the air shimmered with heat. The only way down to the edge of the trees was straight across a marshy stretch of ground. Mosquitoes whined through the air. Storm flicked his ears as the insects darted in to bite where they could.

Tom's heart raced with a mixture of fear and excitement as he clicked his tongue and urged Storm forward. Batting at the insects, they struggled on to the edge of the jungle.

Soon they were facing a dense wall of trees. It was hard to see far into the jungle. Strange screeching sounds could be heard high in the canopy. The air was still and expectant.

"I don't like this," Elenna murmured.

Tom could feel Storm tensing beneath him. He shifted the shield on his arm, bringing it close to his chest. Silver was pacing uncomfortably, his tail low and his ears flattened to his head. It was impossible to ignore the feeling of menace that surrounded the Dark Jungle.

Taking out Aduro's map, Tom studied it once more. The golden dot of the chain mail had moved again. Now it looked very close to where they were standing. Tom squinted into the jungle.

"We have no choice, Elenna," he said, rolling up the map. "We have to go in. We need to defeat all the Beasts and collect every piece of the golden armor before we can rescue Aduro."

Tom thought again about the kindly wizard. He swallowed.

"We *have* to rescue him," he said firmly, and urged Storm forward.

The four travelers took their first step into the jungle. Immediately, Tom noticed the heat. The hot, sticky air made it hard to breathe. He could feel his lungs straining under the pressure.

Storm shook his head nervously; Silver growled softly. Fleshy jungle plants hung all around them. The air was thick with their strange and powerful scents.

"I have never seen plants like these," Elenna said in wonder. She stretched out her hand to touch a red trumpetlike flower.

Immediately the flower snapped closed and, before Elenna could react, snakelike tendrils wrapped themselves around her arm.

"Tom!" she shrieked.

Tom pulled out his sword and slashed the tendrils away. "Touch nothing," he warned, glancing around. He half-expected to see Malvel himself, laughing from the treetops.

The air grew thicker and darker as they pressed on, and the ground became wetter and wetter. Soon Storm was wading cautiously through dark, stinking water, his hooves sliding in the mud, his nostrils flaring at the unfamiliar scents.

"It's OK." Tom soothed and stroked his horse's mane.

Halfway across the swamp, Tom dismounted. He did not want to be responsible for Storm sinking into the uncertain ground. Elenna did the same and pressed ahead with Silver.

The water was unpleasantly warm and sucked at his legs. Gritting his teeth, Tom took Storm's reins and led the stallion gently onward. His eyes darted around, checking for signs of the Beast.

Elenna was waiting for them on the far side of the swamp. With Silver at her side, she was methodically removing the leeches that had attached themselves to her flesh. Then she did the same for Tom and Storm.

They moved on, wet and tired. At last they emerged into a sun-dappled open space.

A group of chattering monkeys suddenly swung down through the vines. Silver barked furiously and Storm reared in surprise.

Tom and Elenna dived to the jungle floor in fright.

"Stay down, Elenna!" Tom said, reaching for his sword.

Chattering among themselves, the monkeys settled in a tree and began grooming each other. Sheepishly, Tom and Elenna got to their feet, laughing nervously.

They moved on, Tom using his sword to slash through the damp green undergrowth.

Suddenly, Elenna stopped. "Look," she said, pointing at a series of deep gashes in the tree trunks.

"Something terrible happened here," Tom said slowly, inspecting several huge chunks gouged out of the undergrowth. Torn branches littered the ground.

Storm gave a high, anxious whinny.

Just then, they heard a rustling behind them. Tom and Elenna whirled around as a claw that was bigger than both of their heads swiped at them from high up in the trees. It was attached to a long, furry tail.

Tom pushed Elenna out of the way, and they tumbled to the ground.

A chill settled in Tom's heart.

It was the Beast. And now the Beast knew they were here.

⤐ Chapter Four ⥆

CLAW ON THE ATTACK

Tom GLANCED UP INTO THE CANOPY OF TREES. It was almost impossible to see anything against the glare of the sun. Leaves rustled and brushed against one another. The Dark Jungle sounded as if it were laughing at its visitors.

A stench of old meat and sweat drifted down through the branches, stronger than the sickly scents of the jungle flowers.

Tom peered again. But it was no use. The Beast was too high up.

"If only I could see more clearly," he said, frustrated. Then he remembered the golden helmet!

Quickly, he pulled it from Storm's saddlebag and put it on, gazing through the slits of the visor up into the treetops again. Now he was able to see the gorgeous greens and vivid colors of the highest point of the jungle.

Then Tom spotted the Beast. He felt his eyes widen in disbelief.

Claw was enormous. His chest was as wide as Storm was long, and his limbs were thicker than some of the tree trunks around them. He sat hunched among the branches, a hideous creature with a lethal-looking claw at the tip of a long, snakelike tail. Huge, hairy arms, legs, hands, and feet ended in vicious, curved claws. His face was covered in matted hair, his squashed snout twisted into an evil snarl. Drool hung in ropes from his long teeth. And his fierce yellow eyes were focused directly on Tom.

There was no choice. They had to run.

"Jump up here, Elenna!" Tom cried, leaping

onto Storm and throwing the helmet back into the safety of the saddlebag.

Elenna flung herself into the saddle behind him, scrabbling for a grip. But before Storm could take them to safety, a torrent of twigs, branches, and vines plunged down from the canopy, knocking Tom and Elenna from the saddle. Claw gave a screech of triumph.

Tom tried to struggle to his feet but the weight of the twisted vines was pressing down on him, like an enormous tangled net.

"I can't move!" Elenna cried.

The more they twisted, the more tightly the vines drew around them. The stink of the Beast was everywhere. Tom's arms were pinned down; he couldn't reach his sword.

Claw screeched again. Then, to Tom's horror, the Beast's long clawed tail swung down and plucked Elenna into the air, ripping the tangled vines away from her with ease.

"Tom!" screamed Elenna.

"No!" Tom cried. He fought to escape, but there was nothing he could do.

Elenna kicked and yelled as the Beast pulled her up into the trees. Her arms flailed, hitting out uselessly at her captor.

Then there was a sudden awful silence. Where had the Beast taken her?

Silver ripped himself free with his teeth before tearing at the vines around Tom.

"That's it, boy!" Tom shouted, struggling to free his arms. "Nearly there!"

At last, he could move his arms. Bursting free, he drew his sword and thrust it into the air.

"While there's blood in my veins," he vowed, "I will save my friend!"

Quickly, he cut away the vines that still bound Storm's legs. The stallion waited patiently as Tom tugged him free.

Claw had left a trail of destruction in his wake —

it would be easy to follow him. But Tom needed a plan.

Picking up the scent of his mistress, Silver threw back his head and started to howl.

"No!" Tom cried, running to the wolf. He patted the animal's thick fur and shushed him. Right now, noise could be deadly.

But it was too late. Behind him, Tom heard a telltale rustling. He looked over his shoulder, hooking a protective arm around Silver.

The Beast's huge shadow spread across the clearing. Claw was back, high in the trees once more. There was no sign of Elenna. Where was he hiding her?

Tom tensed as the clawed tail flew down through the branches once again. He dived out of the way, but the claw violently slapped Silver and Storm to one side, and Tom lost sight of them. He hoped that they were all right, and concentrated on the branches, waiting for the tail to reappear.

It lashed toward him suddenly.

Tom ducked, desperate to evade the cruel claw at its tip. The Beast remained in the trees. It was impossible for Tom to see more than his tail.

Claw gibbered and whirled his tail again. This time, Tom reached out and grabbed hold of it.

"Come down, you coward!" Tom yelled, tugging at the Beast in an effort to bring it crashing to the ground.

The great ape simply lifted his tail. Yanked off his feet, Tom went flying through the air.

Tom clung on with all his strength as Claw's tail whipped and thrashed around. The Beast roared and leaped from tree to tree. Tom swung beneath him, jagged twigs and branches tearing at his clothes. The breath was knocked out of him as the Beast slammed him into trees and dragged him through curtains of vines that scratched his face.

He'd never escape the Dark Jungle alive!

CHAPTER FIVE

FALLING

Tom couldn't hold on much longer. His clothes were torn to shreds. His arms and legs were black with bruises. There was no choice: He had to let go.

Timing it as best he could, Tom released his hold on the Beast's tail and plummeted down through the canopy, twigs snapping in his wake. Stretching out for the nearest tree, his fingers snagged on a branch and he swung there, breathless but safe.

Above him, Claw stood up, thumped his vast chest, and shrieked at the sky. The treetops shook.

His hands scratched and numb, Tom nearly lost

his grip on the branch, but managed to wrap his legs around the tree trunk. For the first time, he saw the whole of Claw as the Beast swung from tree to tree above him. The strange movement of the golden dot on Aduro's map suddenly made sense.

The chain mail was draped around Claw's neck.

Tom gasped with wonder at the sight. The piece of armor shimmered magically. The links seemed too fine to be made of metal, and made Tom think of golden silk knotted into a pattern sparkling in the light.

Suddenly, Claw dropped down through the trees and lunged at Tom again. The Beast's hairy lips were drawn back, revealing his horrible, grinning fangs. Tom grabbed his sword and fought as hard as he could, but it was almost impossible to keep a grip on the tree while he swung his blade.

The clawed tail shot toward him once again. This time, it knocked Tom's sword out of his hand.

Tom watched in horror as his sword spiraled down to the ground and out of sight. Now he was defenseless.

He risked a glance at the jungle floor. It seemed a long way down, but his position on the tree trunk was dangerous. He shifted his shield farther onto his back, trying to get a better grip on the branch.

Think, Tom, he told himself fiercely.

Then it came to him.

In his shield lay the power that Cypher the Mountain Giant had passed on to him. It protected him from great heights.

Pulling his shield from his back, he held it above his head.

Then he took a deep breath and jumped.

Vines and branches whistled past, but Tom felt the power of the shield protecting him. His fall was slowing!

Even so, he hit the ground hard, the wind knocked out of him. Within moments, he was buried in the undergrowth. To his relief, his sword lay nearby. He stretched out a hand and grabbed it.

Claw shrieked once more, and the sound echoed around the jungle. Then silence fell. It seemed that the Beast had given him up for dead.

Tom lay as still as he could, the comforting weight of the sword in his hand. He collected his thoughts and tried to come up with a plan. But where were Storm and Silver? He hadn't seen them since the Beast had knocked them aside with his tail. His heart lurched as he glanced around.

Then he heard Storm neigh. The ground beneath him trembled as the stallion cantered toward him with Silver close at his heels.

Storm nudged him and whinnied.

"Hush," Tom whispered, reaching up and stroking Storm's nose. "I'm all right."

He peered through the leaves over his head. There was nothing in the canopy above him. Tom climbed to his feet. He could hardly believe that he had no broken limbs.

He looked at his shield and offered silent thanks to Avantia's great Beasts who had given him their tokens of power, now set deep into the wooden face of the shield: Ferno's dragon scale protected him from heat, Sepron's tooth from rushing water, and Tartok's claw from extreme cold. Tagus's horseshoe fragment gave him extra speed and Epos's golden feather healed wounds. And, of course, Cypher's single tear, which protected him from great heights, had just saved his life.

Hacking his way free from the undergrowth was almost as difficult as freeing himself from the vines. The ferns of the Dark Jungle were thick and strong, and curled around him.

Then Tom felt something tickling his leg. He looked down.

A snake was coiling around his knee. Its green-brown skin gleamed in the dim jungle light.

Every now and again, a thin black tongue flickered and was gone again. Its yellow eyes were fixed on Tom.

Without taking his eyes off the snake, Tom knocked the creature into the air with the tip of his sword and sliced through its body. The snake's green-brown coils twitched and fell to the ground in two pieces. Tom sighed with relief.

Silver pressed his nose to the ground. His ears pricked and he whined. He had picked up Elenna's scent again!

Tom leaped into Storm's saddle. It was time for battle.

We're coming, Elenna! he thought. *Just hold on!*

Silver took off, following the scent. Broken branches dangled from the trees above them as Tom and Storm galloped through the jungle after the wolf. The Beast had cut a path through the canopy that was easy to follow.

Stumbling and slipping, they raced past trunks

as thick as ten men. Storm darted between trees and beneath vines, taking sharp turns and following the wolf. Alert for signs of danger, Tom watched the trees and clutched his sword.

It wasn't long before the tangle of trees cleared a little. Silver bounded forward and Storm tossed his head, as Tom pressed his heels into the stallion's flanks, encouraging him to gallop faster.

But something was wrong with the path in front of them. The land ahead seemed to be falling away. Storm stiffened as Tom desperately reined him in.

"Silver!" Tom cried. "Look out!"

The wolf twisted his body sharply. But it was too late. Tom watched in horror as Silver went skidding over the edge — and out of sight!

CHAPTER SIX

INTO THE VOLCANO

Tom flung himself off Storm's back and ran to the edge of the precipice. An enormous hole in the ground lay before him. Tom felt a tremor run through his body. He had seen something like this before, when he had freed Epos the Winged Flame from Malvel's curse. Only that had been blazing with lava and smoke. This was rich with plant life.

It was the crater of a vast, extinct volcano.

Tom remembered the horror of his battle to free Epos. He had come close to falling into the boiling lava because he had moved too near the crater's edge, where the ground was loose. This time, he sank to his knees and crawled, just to be safe.

Far below, the heart of the crater was as dark as night. Trees grew tall, reaching up toward the blue sky, desperate for light. It was almost impossible to make out the ground beneath the luxuriant canopy of leaves.

There was no way that Silver could have survived that fall.

But then Tom caught sight of the wolf's silvery pelt. His heart leaped with joy as he saw the wolf crouched below him, on a nearly invisible ledge beneath the lip of the crater. Somehow the wolf had landed there, sparing himself from the deadly fall.

Silver stood on his back legs as Tom reached out to him, nosing thankfully at Tom's hand. The ledge was at an awkward angle, tucked underneath the overhang where Tom lay. Reaching down,

Tom sank his fingers into Silver's thick pelt and heaved with all his might. The wolf scrambled to safety.

"Good boy," Tom murmured, rubbing Silver's head. He felt faint with relief.

The wolf suddenly pulled away from Tom. He ran to the edge of the precipice and sniffed at the air, growling softly.

"What is it?" Tom said, his heart filling with hope.

Silver whined and paced close to the crater, stopping just short of the edge. Stones broke away and bounced down the sheer slope, out of sight.

The golden helmet would help Tom to see what Silver had scented. He ran to Storm and lifted the helmet from the saddlebag once more. Then he placed it on his head and gazed back down at the crater.

He could see brightly colored beetles and sleeping snakes, and every leaf was pinpoint clear. Tom's

eyes swept the ground again. Then, through a crack in the canopy, he spotted Elenna in the gloom at the heart of the crater itself.

She was sitting on the ground, her head in her arms. Scattered around her were piles of gleaming bones. It was Claw's lair!

Tom's head was whirling. He had to defeat Claw and get the chain mail — only by completing the suit of golden armor piece by piece could he rescue Aduro. But first, he needed to save Elenna.

You can do this! Tom told himself. *Take it one step at a time.*

He glanced around, looking for the Beast. He didn't want Claw to know he had found Elenna. Then he gave a long, low whistle to catch his friend's attention. The Beast was less likely to hear him that way.

Elenna looked up. The thick canopy of leaves was blocking her view of Tom. He whistled again.

Getting to her feet, Elenna moved to a piece of clear ground — and grinned with relief when she saw him.

Tom placed a finger on his lips, warning her to stay quiet. He could smell Claw's stench; the Beast wasn't far away. Shadows danced on the ground from the branches high above, playing tricks on Tom's eyes. He whirled around, his eyes darting from shadow to shadow. Where was the giant ape?

At last, Tom spotted him. High in the canopy above Tom's head, Claw's long tail lazily swung back and forth. It looked as if the creature was asleep. The chain mail glimmered and chinked around his neck. The sound made Tom think of tiny bells. His heart quickened. The armor seemed to call out to him, shining softly in the sunlight. Tom hesitated, glancing back at the crater.

Elenna first, he thought.

He looked at the vertical walls of the crater. There was no way down or up. And it was too deep for any of the nearby vines to reach the bottom.

He had no idea how to get Elenna out.

A hissing sound made him look down. Elenna was gesturing something. At last, Tom realized what she wanted — her bow and arrow!

Tom began a careful sweep of the ground where Claw had dragged Elenna to his lair. Silver kept watch at the mouth of the crater while Storm quietly cropped the grass.

At last, Tom spotted the familiar leather quiver holding Elenna's arrows. Beside it lay her bow. They hadn't fallen into the crater but they were teetering dangerously close to the edge.

Tom reached for the weapon, but it was just too far from his grasp. He couldn't creep any closer to the edge, or he would tumble over and all would be lost. He watched in dismay as a gust of wind caused the quiver to gently seesaw over the chasm. There wasn't a moment to lose!

Wrapping one hand around a nearby gum tree, Tom leaned as far as he dared toward the weapons. His fingertips brushed the quiver, but he wasn't close enough to grasp it. He uncurled his fingers slightly from the tree and dug his toes into the damp ground. Just a little farther . . .

Suddenly, Tom felt his fingers slip from the gum tree. His toes scrabbled for a grip, but it was hopeless.

Tom was falling. The Quest was lost.

Aduro! Tom thought. *Aduro, I'm sorry. . . .*

But then, just as he was about to tip over the edge, something grabbed his leg and held him fast. Tom glanced over his shoulder to see Silver gripping his trouser leg in his jaws.

Grasping the bow and arrows firmly in his hand, he rolled back from the edge of the crater with a hammering heart.

"Thank you, Silver," he whispered, throwing his arms around the wolf's strong neck.

He tied the bow and quiver of arrows together with a vine and threw them down to Elenna. Without a word, she took the arrows in her quiver, fitted them to her bow, and began firing them into the walls of the crater.

Everything became clear as Tom watched where the arrows fell. The arrows had formed a ladder up the crater wall that she could climb to safety.

Tom fell back with a gasp of relief. The ground was cool under his back. He knew how lucky he was to have such a quick-thinking companion on this Quest. Elenna would climb out of the sleeping volcano and then they would face Claw.

Together.

CHAPTER SEVEN

FACING THE BEAST

WHEN HE HAD CAUGHT HIS BREATH, TOM glanced up into the canopy. He was wearing the helmet and could see that Claw was still sleeping, his limbs hanging like thick ropes from the branch overhead. They were safe — but there was no way of telling for how long.

He wriggled back to the edge of the crater and watched as Elenna stepped up onto the first arrow. The arrow bent slightly beneath her weight, and she struggled to keep her balance.

Tom cut down a length of vine with his sword. He looped it around a tree trunk and threw the other end to Elenna. It reached halfway down. If she could get there, he could pull her up the rest of the way with a little help from Storm and Silver.

Elenna nodded gratefully, understanding what he was trying to do. But first she had to get to the vine.

Tom looked on with admiration as his friend grasped the arrow above her head, then climbed on to the arrow just below, repeating this movement until she had reached the vine. Each time she took a step up, she reached down to retrieve the arrow she had left behind.

Silver ran back and forth along the mouth of the crater. To Tom's relief, the wolf seemed to know that he should be silent.

Soon, Elenna reached the vine and grabbed the end of it. Together, Tom, Silver, and Storm pulled the vine up the side of the crater. Tom wanted to shout for joy as he felt the grasp of his friend's warm palm.

"We did it!" he whispered fiercely.

They were back together!

But now it was time to face the Beast and retrieve the golden chain mail.

"If I climb into the trees," Tom said in a low voice, "I might take Claw by surprise. It's the only advantage we have."

Elenna nodded, her eyes wide and fearful.

Tom walked to a nearby tree and tested it with his weight.

It was the wrong thing to do.

The tree groaned and started to sway. Then, to Tom's horror, its roots began to pull up through the soft ground.

"It's dead!" Elenna gasped, backing away as the tree began to topple.

Tom grabbed Storm's bridle, Elenna grasped Silver's pelt, and they all ran clear as the tree thundered to the ground.

Then they heard a scream from the canopy.

Claw was awake.

"We just lost our advantage," Elenna panted.

Tom watched with awe as the Beast leaped from tree to tree, screeching and beating his chest.

"I still have to fight him, Elenna," he said. "I have to get the chain mail."

"I know," Elenna replied unhappily. "But be careful!"

Tom tucked the golden helmet back into Storm's saddlebag, then gave Elenna his shield. "Use it to protect yourself," he said, setting foot on the sturdiest tree he could see.

Soon he was climbing high into the canopy, his sword swinging awkwardly by his side. Above him, Claw roared in fury, lashing out with his tail.

Tom ducked behind branches as the Beast's razor-sharp tail whistled toward him. Leaves and twigs rained down on the jungle floor. The tree he was climbing shook and shuddered. Grimly, Tom kept scrambling up, then tucked himself into the cleft of a branch and pulled out his sword, swinging it hard as, once again, the cruel claw whirled toward him.

Then a stroke of pure luck: The base of the branch on which Claw was standing broke away from the tree. Screeching, the Beast fell through the leaves in a flurry of matted fur and thrashing limbs, his face contorted with rage.

But as he fell, he lashed out at Tom's branch.

Tom's heart lurched as the branch splintered beneath him. Instinctively, he reached for his shield — remembering too late that he had given it to Elenna.

Tom fell after the Beast, his arms and legs flailing, and landed on a bed of broken branches.

On the ground, just a few feet away from him, Claw was lurching wildly from side to side, roaring with anger and making a clumsy retreat to the nearest tree trunk. But as soon as he leaped onto the tree, his agility and strength seemed to return.

Frustrated and exhausted, Tom prepared to follow. But before he could move, Elenna grabbed hold of him.

"Tom!" she said, her eyes alight. "Did you see how Claw couldn't keep his balance on the ground?"

"I thought he had been injured in the fall," said Tom as he gazed up at the canopy. "But he seems as strong as ever. Elenna, I don't know how I'm going to do this."

"No," Elenna said. "He wasn't injured. It was his curved claws. They give him no grip on the forest floor. You can't defeat him off the ground — we've both seen how he swings through the trees. But if you can somehow get him on the ground, you'll have a chance. A good one."

Tom glanced up at the Beast. Elenna was right. His curved claws were perfectly adapted for swinging among the treetops. But walking on the ground was another matter.

But how could they coax Claw down to the jungle floor? It was impossible!

Tom was exhausted now. He groaned. There was no way he could do this on his own.

Dimly he heard Aduro's voice in his mind: *"Don't give up hope, Tom. Have you forgotten the help you have with you?"*

Yes! he thought. *I'm not alone. I have the great Beasts of Avantia on my side.*

Without Sepron the Sea Serpent's help, Tom knew that they would never have retrieved the golden helmet from Zepha the Monster Squid. It was time to call on the help of another Beast. And Tom knew exactly whom he needed this time. The thought both thrilled and terrified him. For this Beast was one of the mightiest in all of Avantia.

Ferno the Fire Dragon.

→ CHAPTER EIGHT ←

FERNO RETURNS

Tom seized his shield from Elenna and quickly rubbed the dragon scale set deep into its surface. He felt a rush of exhilaration when he heard Ferno's roar. It filled the air with heat. The sky above the jungle shimmered. Creatures in the darkness of the jungle shrieked in fear and fled.

The mighty dragon of Avantia soared over the jungle canopy, his black leathery wings beating hard and his eyes glowing red in his coal-black face.

Exhilarated at the sight of their old friend, Elenna and Tom watched as smoke began to fill the jungle. The air darkened. Branches crackled. Trees exploded.

Claw was being smoked out!

The Beast screamed in defiance at the dragon. He swung from a branch with one massive arm and beat his chest with the other. But it was a useless display. Ferno swooped again. The blazing fires gleamed on his polished scales. Claw bellowed and fled through the canopy.

Ferno flew above the giant ape, following his progress through the branches. The dragon's tail struck the trees and brought them crashing down in the giant ape's path. Screeching parrots fluttered into the air, their colors dulled by the smoke. Everywhere, the tops of the trees were burning.

"Go, Ferno!" Elenna screamed.

Tom willed the dragon on with all his heart.

Claw was struggling for breath, his chest heaving. He held his great curved claws over his head, batting uselessly at the smoke. It was everywhere, curling and billowing through the sky. The only place that remained smoke-free was the jungle floor. In desperation, Claw dropped to the ground, snarling.

As soon as the Beast hit the dirt, Tom struck. Claw stumbled, trying to get away, but his clawed feet weren't quick enough. Tom gave chase, leaping through the undergrowth. The Beast hobbled pitifully, stumbling and groaning.

Elenna unleashed a volley of arrows. Claw howled in pain.

"Go, Silver!" she shouted.

The wolf nipped at the Beast's legs in a whirl of silver fur, and Storm joined the fight, his hooves sharp and deadly.

With the help of his friends, Tom closed the gap between himself and the Beast.

Claw was cornered.

Tom thrust hard with his sword, aiming for the

clasp on the golden chain mail, which was hanging around the Beast's neck.

But Claw was not helpless after all. The great clawed tail slashed through the air and flicked him away. Tom tried again. And again the Beast's tail knocked him away. No matter how Tom approached, he could not reach the chain mail with his sword.

Desperate to distract the Beast, Tom whistled sharply for Storm. As the stallion crashed through the foliage, Claw reared back — and Tom seized his chance. He raced up close and leaped onto a branch to raise himself to the level of the Beast's neck. Then, in the blink of an eye, he slid the tip of his sword into the chain mail's clasp and pulled. It half-opened.

Then the Beast's eyes flicked back to Tom and he lunged forward, wrapping his tail around Tom's waist. The tail's grip grew tighter as Tom struggled.

He could feel his insides being crushed. His sword arm was pinned to his side, the weapon useless. The Beast prepared to leap once again into the few remaining trees that weren't yet burning.

"No!" Tom bellowed helplessly.

Then he heard Storm whinny a high-pitched challenge and turned to see Elenna galloping toward him on the black stallion, a splintered tree branch in her hand. She aimed the sharp tip of the branch at Claw, and hurled it like a javelin. It crashed into the half-open clasp on the chain mail and loosened it further.

Claw's grip slackened for a moment and Tom pried himself free. He crashed back onto the jungle floor, gulping deep breaths of air. There was no time to check for injuries. Every second counted.

Claw had dropped from the trees again. Screaming at Tom, the hideous Beast's tail whipped through the air.

"Ferno!" Tom shouted in desperation, holding his shield above his head.

The huge scaled head of the fire dragon darted down through the trees. Tom caught a glimpse of a blood-red eye. A jet of fire plumed from Ferno's mouth, bounced off the shield, and hurtled toward Claw.

The giant ape pulled up his tail and leaped back, screaming in fear, as Ferno's flames consumed the ground in front of him. The shield protected Tom from the heat, but he and his friends would soon be choked by the smoke.

"Again, Ferno!" Tom called, as his eyes stung and watered in the thick gray air.

Ferno roared, and there was another jet of bright flame. Tom almost fell backward as the force of the fire hurtled into the shield and changed direction — straight toward Claw.

→ CHAPTER NINE ←

VICTORY

CLAW SCREECHED, LURCHING AWAY FROM THE flames. There was nowhere left for him to go. The trees all around were burning, opening great charred gaps to the sky. The Beast fell to his knees. Tom threw himself at Claw's exposed neck and tore open the loosened clasp. At last, the golden chain mail slithered to the ground.

Ferno's roar shook the jungle. One last column of fire, as wide as a tree trunk, blasted into the ground, hiding Claw behind a thick black cloud of smoke.

Stiffly, Tom reached for his sword again, ready to protect everything that he held dear.

The smoke began to clear. But where the great shaggy body of Claw should have been, something extraordinary met Tom's eyes.

A group of small, excitable monkeys were clustered together on the ground. They chattered, jumped into the lower branches of the unburned trees, and happily groomed each other.

Where had the Beast gone?

Elenna looked as puzzled as Tom felt. He gazed again at the empty space where Claw had cowered just a few seconds earlier. Then he stared back at the trees where the monkeys were sitting. He'd never seen anything quite like it before.

He collapsed to his knees, his lungs suddenly raw: It was all over. Dimly, he heard Elenna's voice.

"Tom!" she called. "Tom, you've done it!"

Ferno gave a piercing cry. Tom looked up. Above the burned wreckage of the Dark Jungle, the vast wings of the dragon were beating.

"Thank you, Ferno," he whispered.

The dragon cried again, a sweet, fierce sound that Tom knew he would never forget. As Tom watched, he swooped away. Soon, Ferno was no more than a black speck in the distance.

The next thing he saw was Elenna's face, grimy and bright with triumph.

"The chain mail, Tom!" she said. "It's yours!"

Climbing slowly to his feet, Tom stumbled over to the golden chain mail, the second piece of the precious armor. It was warm to the touch. He lifted it up, almost staggering at its weight. For a moment, he panicked. It was too heavy. He would never be able to lift it over his shoulders.

But as he did, the links slithered into place. Immediately, Tom became aware of a magic pulse in his chest, and the chain mail felt as light as a feather. Energy surged into his tired muscles. He felt as brave as a lion.

He looked at Elenna, who was standing in the clearing with Storm and Silver at her side. "Extra strength of heart," he murmured, stroking the chain mail. "The helmet gives me sharper sight, and the chain mail makes me feel as if I could face any battle. I could fight ten new Beasts right now, Elenna. Twenty!"

Elenna grinned. "Well done, Tom."

"I would never have called Ferno if you hadn't suggested that we had to fight Claw on the ground," Tom admitted.

"Hey," said Elenna, looking pleased. "I always knew I was the brains of this team."

Storm whinnied softly and pushed at Tom's hand. Tom stroked the stallion's dusty black coat as Silver lay panting at Elenna's feet.

Then he took off the chain mail and laid it gently across Storm's back. Tiredness seeped back into his muscles. "Now I could sleep for a week," he said. "But we still have more pieces of armor to find, and more Beasts to defeat. And Aduro . . ."

His voice trailed away. Soberly, Elenna met his gaze. Was King Hugo's wizard still alive? Was he holding out against Malvel's evil magic?

"We must leave this place," Tom said. "We have to finish the Quest as quickly as we can so that we can rescue Aduro."

They began walking back the way they had come. Everything looked different, blackened and twisted by the force of Ferno's fire.

Soon they reached the thick green trees in the heart of the Dark Jungle. Ferno's flames had not touched this place. They moved slowly through the maze of plants and vines. Monkeys, small and unthreatening, chattered and swung through the branches above them.

"Watch out for snakes," Tom warned Elenna,

remembering the snake he had killed. "They are everywhere."

Suddenly, there was a strange thickening in the air.

"You'll have to watch out for more than that," came a mocking voice.

Tom gasped. He reached for his sword as a shimmering image of Malvel appeared against the canopy of leaves above them.

"We have two pieces of the golden armor, Malvel!" Tom shouted defiantly. "We defeated Claw! It won't be long before we find you and rescue Aduro — and then there will be nothing you can do."

"You will not be so sure of yourself when you meet the next evil Beast — Soltra," said Malvel.

"Where is Aduro?" Tom challenged.

Malvel laughed, a sneering sound that echoed around the jungle. His image faded. In his place,

Tom saw the great jungle crater they had left behind. Lying among the white animal bones was a scrap of red cloth.

"Aduro's cloak is red," said Elenna, her voice filled with anger. "What have you done with him, Malvel? If you have harmed him . . ."

The sound of Malvel's laughter filled the air once more as the image of the crater receded, and Tom felt something brush past him. He whirled around, but could see nothing.

"Good luck," the voice of Malvel whispered in his ear. It felt like the cold touch of a bat's wing. "You and your team of nobodies. When you see what still lies in store on this Quest, you'll need it. . . ."

Tom gripped his sword, feeling the comforting weight of his shield on his back. He remembered the golden helmet in Storm's saddlebag and glanced at the golden chain mail that lay across the stallion's broad back. They were not alone. The

Beasts of Avantia were on their side, and with every evil Beast he defeated he gained one more piece of the precious armor. His powers were growing.

"We'll be ready!" he vowed, thrusting his sword into the air. "Whatever it takes, Malvel, we will defeat you!"

THE SECRETS OF DROON

By Tony Abbott

Under the stairs, a magical world awaits you!

Over 6.7 Million copies sold!

SCHOLASTIC

www.scholastic.com/droon

DROONBL2